A NOTE TO PARENTS

When your children are ready to "step into reading," giving them the right books is as crucial as giving them the right food to eat. **Step into Reading Books** present exciting stories and information reinforced with lively, colorful illustrations that make learning to read fun, satisfying, and worthwhile. They are priced so that acquiring an entire library of them is affordable. And they are beginning readers with a difference—they're written on five levels.

Early Step into Reading Books are designed for brand-new readers, with large type and only one or two lines of very simple text per page. **Step 1 Books** feature the same easy-to-read type as the Early Step into Reading Books, but with more words per page. **Step 2 Books** are both longer and slightly more difficult, while **Step 3 Books** introduce readers to paragraphs and fully developed plot lines. **Step 4 Books** offer exciting nonfiction for the increasingly independent reader.

The grade levels assigned to the five steps—preschool through kindergarten for the Early Books, preschool through grade 1 for Step 1, grades 1 through 3 for Step 2, grades 2 through 3 for Step 3, and grades 2 through 4 for Step 4—are intended only as guides. Some children move through all five steps very rapidly; others climb the steps over a period of several years. Either way, these books will help your child "step into reading" in style!

ISBN 0-439-22202-8

Text copyright © 1998 by Deborah Hautzig. Illustrations copyright © 1998 by Sylvie Wickstrom. All rights reserved. Published by Scholastic Inc., 555 Broadway, New York, NY 10012, by arrangement with Random House Children's Books, a division of Random House, Inc. STEP INTO READING is a registered trademark of Random House, Inc. SCHOLASTIC and associated logos are trademarks and/or registered trademarks of Scholastic Inc.

12 11 10 9 8   9 10 11 12 13/0

Printed in the U.S.A.   23

First Scholastic printing, September 2000

Step into Reading®

Little Witch Goes to School

A Step 2 Book

By Deborah Hautzig

Illustrated by Sylvie Wickstrom

For my fabulous friend,
Fran Manushkin
—D. H.

SCHOLASTIC INC.
New York Toronto London Auckland Sydney
Mexico City New Delhi Hong Kong

Little Witch was bored.

There was nobody to play with

except her cat, Bow-Wow,

and her bat, Scrubby.

And they were bored, too.

Little Witch went into the kitchen.

There was Mother Witch,

making spaghetti and mouseballs.

"There is nobody to play with,"

Little Witch told Mother Witch.

"Everybody is starting

school today—except me.

I'm *bored*. I miss my friends."

"Good!" said Mother Witch.

"I like it when you complain.

"Go find Aunt Nasty
and Aunt Grouchy.
Maybe they can
teach you to be mean."
"I'm not very good
at being mean,"
said Little Witch.
"Well, TRY HARDER!"
screamed Mother Witch.

Aunt Nasty was on the roof
with Aunt Grouchy.
They were throwing
smelly old eggs
at the mailman.
"You always bring JUNK!"
screamed Aunt Nasty.
Little Witch felt sorry
for him.

She said a magic spell:

"Soapy dopey,

Eggy free,

You're as clean

As clean can be!"

ZAP! The mailman was clean.

"Party pooper!"

shrieked Aunt Grouchy.

"Go away, Little Witch!"

Little Witch went
back inside.
"Aunt Grouchy told me to go away.
What can I do now,
Mother Witch?"
"Go find Cousin Dippy,"
said Mother Witch.
"She is always doing
something stupid.
Maybe you can help."

Cousin Dippy was in the yard.

"The leaves are

falling off the tree!

So I'm taping them back on."

"Cousin Dippy doesn't

understand about Fall,"

Little Witch whispered

to Bow-Wow.

"The leaves are *supposed*

to fall off."

Little Witch went

into the kitchen again.

"Can I *please* go to school?"

she begged.

"No! And NEVER say PLEASE!"

yelled Mother Witch.

"What if I promise to be good?"

asked Little Witch.

"You are ALREADY too good!"

screamed Mother Witch.

"Okay," said Little Witch quietly.

"What if I promise to be *bad?*"

Mother Witch looked up.

Her witchy eyes twinkled.

"Deal!" said Mother Witch.

The next morning,
Little Witch got ready for school.
Aunt Grouchy and Aunt Nasty
gave her a wormy apple
for the teacher.
Cousin Dippy gave her
a box of crayons.
Mother Witch gave her
a lunchbox full of candy.
"This will help your teeth rot,"
she said.

"Remember to be bad!

Don't make any new friends!

And DON'T LEARN ANYTHING!"

"I'll try, Mother Witch,"

said Little Witch.

"See you later, everybody!"

When Little Witch got to school,

she saw her friends

Milly, Sam, and Marcus.

"Here I am!" said Little Witch.

The teacher's name

was Ms. Brooks.

She was shocked to see
Little Witch in her classroom.
But she was very polite.
"We have a new student today,"
she told the class.
"Can you tell her your names?"
One by one, everyone
said their names.

"Why are you dressed
as a witch, dear?"
asked Ms. Brooks.
She looked worried.
"Because I *am* a witch,"
said Little Witch proudly.
"But there are no *real* witches,"
said Ms. Brooks.
"Oh, yes, there are!" cried Milly.
"Show her, Little Witch!"

So Little Witch said
a magic spell:
 "Flippety dippety,
   Witch's broom,
   Watch me fly
   Around this room!"

WHOOSH!
Little Witch flew
around and around
the classroom.

Ms. Brooks gasped.

She had never seen

a real witch before.

"That's amazing!" cried Cherry.

"Can you teach us to fly, too?"

"WHAT?" shrieked Ms. Brooks.

"Don't worry," said Little Witch.

"I will take everyone for a ride—

after school.

School is much more fun

than flying!"

Ms. Brooks was very relieved

to hear *that*.

"Here is an apple for you,

Ms. Brooks,"

said Little Witch.

Suddenly the worms popped out.

Ms. Brooks screamed.

"I'll fix it in a jiffy,"

said Little Witch.

She said these magic words:

"Junky monkey,

Stinkeroozer,

This old apple

Is a loser!"

POOF! The wormy apple

was gone.

In its place was a banana.

"I hope you like bananas,"

said Little Witch.

Little Witch looked
around the classroom.
Each child had a cubby
to put things in.
"This cubby is yours,"
Ms. Brooks told Little Witch.

"Wow," said Little Witch.

"I never had a cubby before."

"And I never had a little witch

in my class before!"

said Ms. Brooks.

"You do now,"

said Little Witch happily.

"Everyone sit in a circle,"
said Ms. Brooks.
"Whose job is it to
feed the fish today?"
"Cherry and Mary,"
said Marcus.
"They like to do things together,"
he told Little Witch.

"What will my job be?"

asked Little Witch.

"You may clean up

the floor after art class,"

said Ms. Brooks.

"Thank you!" cried Little Witch.

"I love to clean up!"

Job chart

Cherry

Mar

Mi

Sar

Art came next.

Ms. Brooks let everyone

draw pictures.

Little Witch used her crayons

from Cousin Dippy.

But something was not right.

"Oh, dear," said Little Witch.

"The blue one draws in green.

The green one draws in purple.

The yellow one draws in blue.

They're all mixed up—

just like Cousin Dippy."

"I'll trade you," said Willie.

"Your crayons are much

more fun."

"Deal!" said Little Witch.

"I always wanted real crayons."

When it was time to clean up,

Little Witch said

some magic words:

"Ickety stickety,

Messy floor,

You're as clean

As you were before!"

POOF! The floor was clean.

Everyone clapped—

even Ms. Brooks.

After art,

it was time to eat lunch.

"Look what Little Witch has

in her lunchbox!" cried Mary.

"It's candy!" cried Cherry.

"Yes," said Little Witch sadly.

"Mother Witch always

gives me candy for lunch."

"Let's trade," said Cherry.

"If you give us your candy,

we will each give you

half a sandwich."

"Deal!" said Little Witch happily.

"I never get a sandwich

for lunch!"

After lunch came recess.
Ms. Brooks let everyone
play in the yard.
Cherry and Mary and Willie
and Walter showed Little Witch
how to play games
she had never played before.
They played hopscotch…and tag…
and hide-and-seek…
and Simon says.

In the afternoon,

Ms. Brooks read a story out loud.

It was about a tiny girl

named Thumbelina.

Then the children made up

their own story.

It was about a tiny boy

named Pinky.

Ms. Brooks wrote down the words.

"Tomorrow we can make

our own book," said Ms. Brooks.

"Great idea!" said Esther.

All the children agreed.

Then it was time to go home.

"Once upon a time, there was a tiny boy named Pinky."

Little Witch was so sorry

that school was over!

She began to cry.

"Don't worry," said Ms. Brooks.

"You can come back tomorrow."

Little Witch stopped crying.

"I forgot about tomorrow.

I feel much better now.

Good-bye, everybody!"

"WAIT!" cried Cherry.

"You promised us a ride!"

"Oops! You're right,"

said Little Witch.

"But first, we need

an extra-long broomstick."

Little Witch said:

"Roomy broomy,

Stringy cheese,

I need a ten-foot

Broomstick, please!"

In a flash,

she was holding

the longest broomstick ever.

"Hop on!" said Little Witch.

"Now we need a flying spell,"

said Little Witch.

She said:

"Twinkle dinkle,

Frenchy fry,

Now we're flying

In the sky!"

With a loud WHOOSH,

they took off.

They flew over towns

and around tall buildings...

They flew over the ocean...

They flew all the way to Paris....

And then they flew

over and under

London Bridge!

At last—THUMP!

They landed in front of

Little Witch's house.

There was Mother Witch,

waiting on the porch.

"Who are all these children?"

said Mother Witch.

"These are my friends

from school!"

said Little Witch.

"I TOLD you not to
make any friends!"
screamed Mother Witch.
"Send them home,
and GO TO BED!"
Little Witch said a spell:
  "Snuggly wuggly,
   Sleepyheads,
   Zap my friends
   Into their beds."
POOF! Her friends were gone.
Little Witch felt very sad.

POOF!

Mother Witch came into

Little Witch's room.

Little Witch hid under the covers.

"You broke your promise,"

said Mother Witch.

"I know," said Little Witch.

"It's *bad* to break a promise,"

said Mother Witch.

"I know," said Little Witch.

Then Mother Witch smiled
and said, "You see?
You were bad after all!
I'm proud of you,
Little Witch."

Mother Witch hugged Little Witch.

"Good night," said Mother Witch.

"I hope you have
lots of bad dreams."
But Little Witch
had good dreams all night
about her wonderful day
at school.